BURGERS AND BODIES

Day and Night Diner, Book 2

GRETCHEN ALLEN

Summer Prescott Books Publishing

CHAPTER ONE

Josslyn Rockwell was a career waitress. She'd been working the same job waiting tables for the last fifteen years, and before that, she worked at a truck stop in a nearby town. Many people in her life, including her family, thought it was a strange career choice, but for Joss, she couldn't be happier. She loved everything about the Day and Night Diner, especially her crazy customers and even crazier coworkers.

Layering slices of tomato and red onion on the top half of a sesame seed bun, Joss made sure the presentation of the food looked perfect before carrying it out to her table.

"What did you say this was called again?" the older man asked.

"A Juicy Lucy, dear. She called it a Juicy Lucy." The woman across from him, likely his wife, rolled her eyes.

"Well, that's quite the name." The man chortled.

Joss stifled a laugh. Every time the diner had a Juicy Lucy as a lunch special, someone had jokes. It wasn't as though they'd created the name themselves or anything. Juicy Lucy burgers had been around for years. The burger, stuffed with cheese, rather than having it melted on top, was a favorite of many, despite the somewhat comical name.

"It certainly is," Joss agreed. "Can I get the two of you anything else?"

"How about something for us to dip our burgers in? Not ketchup or anything; something that would go well with whatever is stuffed inside," the man requested.

"Hmm. Well, since they are stuffed with bacon and bleu cheese tossed in buffalo sauce, what about ranch dressing? That might tame the heat factor a little," Joss suggested.

"Sounds great. Thank you."

Joss made her way to the kitchen, stopping at a few tables on her way by. Thankfully, things weren't as busy as they could be. Luke, her boss, and the owner of the Day and Night Diner, was outside in the parking lot. He was having one of his obligatory meetings with his best friend that were held in his vehicle, so he'd left Joss to her own devices. She'd spent the late morning working in the kitchen and waiting tables. It was the time between breakfast and lunch rush, so things were relatively slow and tolerable on her own.

Once she'd dropped off the ranch dressing to her table, Joss did her best to tidy things up for when Dina arrived. While it wasn't necessary, she always tried to make sure that everything was just how Dina liked it. Sometimes her coworker liked to fancy herself the manager of the diner. That couldn't be farther from the truth, but no one ever seemed to have anything to say about it. As if on cue, Dina burst through the front door of the diner, stopping in her tracks the moment she crossed the threshold.

"Hello, Joss," Dina spoke, seemingly out of breath.

"Is everything okay?" Joss asked, eyeing Dina. "Why are you covered in feathers?"

3

"If you must know," she said, pulling a feather from her forearm, "I got caught in the rain and had to put on this embarrassing dress my mother sent me. I've had it in my car sitting in the same box it came in for months. I'm mortified to even be seen in something so preposterous."

Joss looked Dina over. She had on red platform wedges, and a solid black sundress, both of which looked completely normal to Joss. In fact, she thought Dina looked great, and for once, completely reasonably dressed.

"Yes. That dress. I'm so sorry you have to be seen wearing something so hideous." Joss nodded her head furiously. "But what about the feathers?"

"My boa got soaked, and when I tried taking it off, the feathers were stuck all over me, and it was a huge to-do. I ended up snapping one of my favorite suspenders and had to put this monstrosity on in the meantime. I don't even match a bit. Thankfully, I accidentally left my work clothes here the other day, so I won't have to run home to change."

The funny thing about Dina was that she never accidentally left a change of clothes at work. Joss didn't think Dina ever did anything accidentally. Her outfits were by far some of the strangest she'd ever seen, but Dina didn't seem to recognize that. Joss was determined to figure out what the story behind Dina was, but until then, she'd just go with the flow and humor her coworker.

"Mmhhmm, thankfully is right. I'll cover for you while you change," Joss offered, trying not to laugh.

"Do you think you'll be okay without me?" Dina asked, looking around.

"I'm sure I'll be fine." Joss nodded, not letting the fact that Dina was still standing there, and there were only three customers in the building, go unnoticed.

A few moments later, Dina was back and in her jeans and t-shirt with the Day and Night Diner logo emblazoned on the back.

"Thanks for covering for me," Dina said as though she'd been gone for hours. "Anything interesting happen this morning?"

"Not really," Joss said, thinking about how the most interesting thing was Dina coming in looking like Big Bird. "Luke's outside with Richie and has been for a while, so I've just been doing what I gotta do."

"Before we get busy, there's something I wanted to ask you," Dina said, coming closer.

"What's up?" Joss asked, standing over the grill and flipping a burger patty.

"I'm having a bit of a gathering in a couple of days, and I was wondering if you'd be interested in coming?" Dina rocked back and forth on her heels, not making eye contact.

"I'd love that," Joss said, smiling.

"Really? You mean it?" Dina looked up.

"Of course. I think it sounds great. Just let me know the time and the place, and I'll be there."

Just as Joss was about to pull out her phone to note the details, Luke and Richie entered the diner through the kitchen door. Both men were belly laughing, Richie stopping the moment he saw Dina.

"Hi, Dina," Richie said.

"Hi," Dina replied, turning in the other direction, all but jogging into the dining room.

If Joss didn't know better, she'd say the two of them had something going on. Every time they were around one another, they both acted much more awkward than usual. Richie was a good guy, a little odd, but that wasn't any different from Dina. He spent most of his time hunting for antiques. Joss wasn't entirely sure, but she thought that was Richie's only means of income. He was constantly traveling around Lemon Bay and the surrounding towns. Sometimes he'd be gone for weeks at a time while he left the state in search for the next best thing. Joss could always tell when Richie wasn't around because Luke always spent more time at the diner.

"Hi, Richie," Joss said. "Nice to see you."

"Oh, yeah. Joss. How's it going?" Richie answered absentmindedly, still watching Dina through the doorway.

"Good." She chuckled.

"Can I get you anything to eat?" Luke asked.

"Bacon-Cheddar Juicy Lucy, medium-well with a side of crispy fries. Add some cheese on the fries, too, please," Richie said, finally taking his eyes off Dina long enough to take a seat on his favorite stool.

"Got it," Luke called from the kitchen.

Joss let Luke takeover on the grill and went back out to the dining room to check on her customers. Everyone looked happy; everyone except for Dina who looked like she was about to hyperventilate. Richie was trying to engage her in conversation, and it didn't look like it was going well. Dina could be so bold sometimes, and so hard to get along with, so watching her struggle to make conversation with Richie was more humor than Joss could take.

"Whatcha guys talking about?" Joss asked, inserting herself into their conversation, hoping she'd eased Dina's fluttery heart just a little.

CHAPTER TWO

"Listen, you two," Luke said, calling over Joss and Dina. "A lady called yesterday after you both left wanting some information about a last-minute catering gig. She's gonna call back in a while, and I don't much care which one of you handles it, but as always, let's make sure we go above and beyond. It's good for business and all that jazz."

"I'll do it," Dina said, raising her hand.

That didn't surprise Joss. If there was a catering event and Dina was available, she took it. That was okay with her. Joss did better in tips working at the diner than she did getting paid hourly doing catering jobs, anyway. Plus, she was going to have to cancel her plans with Dina for the following evening, and she didn't want to make things worse by taking the catering call, too. It wasn't like Joss wanted to cancel. She just didn't have much of a choice. Her landlord had called last night and requested a meeting with her, which basically never happened. She only saw him once or twice a year, or if something came up and she needed something repaired. He didn't live in the area, so when he said he wanted to meet with her, she figured it was something important.

"Joss, is that okay with you?" Luke asked.

"Of course. Dina can totally take care of it. I don't mind at all," Joss answered.

"Good. Great." Luke nodded. "On that note, I have to go do payroll."

"I'm looking forward to tomorrow," Dina said once Luke left the kitchen.

"About that," Joss began.

"Don't tell me. Don't even say it," Dina pleaded.

"I'm sorry. It's just that my landlord…"

"I told you not to say it." Dina glared at her.

Joss hadn't really said anything yet, but Dina knew

what she was about to say, and clearly, it wasn't going over very well.

"Dina. Let me make it up to you. I know it won't be the same, but we can go out a different night. You can come to my house or..."

Once again, Dina didn't let her finish. "There won't be a different night. It's fine. Don't worry about it. Don't even let it cross your mind again."

Joss stood there watching as Dina stormed off. She knew Dina was upset. Joss wasn't completely positive, but she didn't think that Dina had very many friends, so this may have hit her a little harder than Joss had expected. If there was a way to make it up to Dina, she was going to figure it out.

"Hey, you," Bridget said, walking in the front door of the diner.

"Hi!" Joss smiled, taken away from her thoughts of Dina. "What are you doing here? Don't you usually have the dogs this time of day?"

Bridget was an old friend of Joss's that she'd recently reconnected with. She was Lemon Bay's official dog walker extraordinaire, or at least that's what Joss liked to call her. Bridget always had someone's dog with her.

"I do. They're outside. I just came in for a quick cup of coffee to go," Bridget explained. "Actually, make it two."

"You left them outside alone? Is that okay to do?" Joss asked.

"I have someone with me today." Bridget grinned. "I hired someone! Do you believe it? I hired an employee!"

"Wow!" Joss said, setting the to-go cups on the counter. "That's really great. I had no idea that you were busy enough to need an employee."

"We're still working out the kinks, but so far so good. I could probably handle it on my own, but I like the idea of having someone else, just in case, ya know?"

"Like for the times you want to run in for a coffee?" Joss joked.

"Exactly." Bridget laughed, handing her a five-dollar bill. "Keep the change. Oh, and by the way, the shelter is having an adoption event soon, you should really consider making a trip there to check out the animals."

Joss wasn't sure that was a very good idea. She worked a lot and didn't think it would be fair to the animal if she were to be gone the majority of the day. But she did love animals.

"Thanks. I'll give it some thought," she told her friend.

"Have a good day!" Bridget called over her shoulder.

Joss was proud of her friend. Hiring an employee was a big deal, and she hoped it worked out.

"Joss! Joooossssssss!" Luke bellowed from the office.

Rolling her eyes, Joss headed toward the booming voice. She never understood why people had to yell across the diner to get someone's attention. It may be a casual place, but that didn't mean they had to act as though they were sitting in their own living room watching a football game.

"Yes?" she asked, looking at Luke, who was surrounded by papers.

"How many hours did you work last week? I can't find anything in this mess."

"Forty-five at the diner and six catering," Joss answered after verifying the times she'd saved on her phone.

"How many of the diner hours were cooking?" Luke asked.

"Uhhh. I'm not sure. I don't really keep track of that anymore," Joss answered.

"Well, you need to start again. Every time you cover for me, especially when you're serving too, I want you to keep track of the hours. Make a note on the time card, or if you can figure out how to clock in as a kitchen employee, do that. I'll be paying you a higher hourly pay for when you're cooking." Luke took his eyes away from his desk to look at Joss.

"You don't have to do that."

"Yes, I do. It's only fair. You help me out way more than you have to and I appreciate it. It may be a little harder to keep track of, but all of your cooking hours will be paid at a higher rate, even if you are here waiting tables. Got it?" Luke asked.

"Got it," Joss said, grinning.

Waitresses made a meager hourly wage because they

relied on their tips as their primary source of income. Joss did well in tips, and that was partially because she knew all of her customers so well and had been doing the job for a long time. She earned a decent living as it was, so finding out that she'd be making more was the icing on the cake. With her luck, though, the meeting with her landlord was because he was raising her rent, and the extra money she'd be earning would go straight to that.

CHAPTER THREE

"Thanks for agreeing to this," Becky said.

"No problem," Joss mumbled, pouring herself some coffee.

Becky, the overnight waitress, had called the diner the day before, minutes before Joss left for the day, asking if she could come in early the following morning. Joss reluctantly agreed since four a.m. wasn't exactly an ideal time to arrive at work, or anywhere for that matter, but Becky would do it for her, so she saw no other option.

"Are sure about that?" Becky laughed.

"I'll be fine." Joss blinked, her eyes adjusting to the bright kitchen lights.

"Do you know what's up with Dina?" Becky asked.

"What do you mean?"

"When I got here last night, she was still here. She had a pad of sticky notes and was frantically writing and sticking them all over. I tried asking what was happening, but she just told me that they weren't for me," Becky said, pointing out a few of the notes.

Joss was speechless. Becky wasn't kidding. There were no less than a dozen pink sticky notes stuck on the shelf behind the counter. Some of the notes had directions on them, which was odd enough on its own. No one that worked at the diner needed instructions on how to do things. It was the notes that were written specifically to Joss that stood out the most. *Don't forget the lunch reservation at noon. I'm coming in early to help. It's a large group, and you'll need it.* Another said, *Please don't accept any phone calls about catering. Take a message, and I'll return the calls.*

"You've got to be kidding," Joss said, shaking her head.

"Why the notes? Is that how she communicates now?" Becky asked. "Not that I'm complaining. Notes are definitely an easier way to talk to her, but she said they weren't for me, and she knew you were coming in next. What happened?"

"I think she's mad at me," Joss explained.

"Ya think?" Becky giggled. "I'm heading out and wishing you luck."

The first two hours after Becky left were quiet. There'd only been a handful of customers, and Joss thanked her lucky stars that she didn't work the overnight shift often. Once six o'clock hit, the diner came to life.

"Good morning," Jack said, entering the diner and passing the newspaper to Joss.

"Morning. I've got your coffee on the table, and blue-berry bagel going already." Joss rested the paper on the counter.

"What if I wanted something else today?" Jack raised a brow and sat down at his regular table.

"Do you?"

"Of course not. Why would you ask something so absurd?" Jack chuckled, looking at the table behind him.

Normally, Hazel Hadley sat there, but she was out of town visiting her children. Saving Jack from having to ask, she let him know that Hazel wouldn't be coming in for the remainder of the week.

"Here's your bagel. Do you want more coffee?" Joss asked.

"I'm good for today. Just one cup will be fine."

"Everything okay?" Joss sat on the stool closest to Jack's table.

"Seems a little quiet in here today, doesn't it?" he mused.

"So far." Joss nodded.

She knew he was referring to Hazel not being there, but didn't want to point it out. Jack and Hazel had an interesting relationship. It was routine for them to meet at the diner, sit at different tables, and have a light and comical bickering session every weekday morning. Some people thrived on routine, and Joss thought Jack might be one of those people.

"Thanks for the meal," Jack said, getting up. "I think I'm going to head out a bit early today. I hear it might rain and I came without my umbrella."

That was all Joss needed to hear. Her suspicions had been confirmed, even more so when she saw Jack pick up his umbrella from just outside the front door. He walked a mile to the diner each morning and never came without his umbrella. Joss thought it was sweet that Jack missed Hazel and told a little fib about why he was leaving early. She may not be much of a matchmaker, but Joss was determined to at least try to get the two of them together. She thought they'd make a great couple.

The next few hours were much busier. Joss didn't have time to think about anything other than serving tables. Luckily, Garth, one of the cooks, was working with her, so she wasn't trying to juggle multiple tasks at the same time. Jack had been right. It was a rainy morning, and that always made the diner busier. For whatever reason, rain made people hungry.

Joss glanced at the clock, seeing that it was about time for Ryan to come in. Ryan Leclair was not only a regular customer but also someone that Joss had gone on a few dates with. There had always been somewhat of an attraction between her and Ryan, similar to Jack and Hazel, but far less strange. After a long cycle of Ryan asking her out and her saying no,

Joss finally sucked it up and asked him out herself. So far, it had been a great decision, because things were going really well. When the front door creaked open, Joss expected to see Ryan walking through the door.

"Do I wait to be seated, or...?" the woman asked.

"Sit wherever you like!" Joss tried to hide her disappointment.

"Thanks," the woman said, looking around for the perfect spot, finally settling on a table near the windows.

"I'm Joss. I'll be taking care of you today," Joss paused, realizing the woman wasn't paying attention. "Ma'am. Can I get you something to drink?"

"Coffee, please," the woman said, staring out the window.

Sometimes customers didn't want to make conversation. Some didn't even say hello to her. While she didn't necessarily enjoy people like that, Joss never let it get to her.

"Sure thing. Are you ready to order, or would you like a few minutes?" Joss asked.

"Just get me the peanut butter and banana pancakes. Lots of syrup too, please." The woman finally looked away from the window, her face red and eyes puffy.

"Of course. I have just the thing."

Joss knew that look. Working in a diner, she saw people come in and out who were upset about one thing or another. Maybe she lost her job or was in a fight with her best friend. Joss would likely never know why the customer was upset, but she'd make sure that her meal was satisfying.

Joss went into the kitchen and told Garth to make two extra fluffy peanut butter banana pancakes and that she'd do the rest. Once the pancakes were done, Joss piled them high with whipped cream, more bananas, both peanut butter, and chocolate chips, and then pulled out her personal stash of chocolate maple syrup. It was her absolute favorite, and she always shared it with people that were having a bad day. Joss poured some into a small dish and rested it next to the pancakes.

"Here we go," she said, setting down the plate.

"Oh, wow," the woman said. "What is all of this?"

"Hopefully just what you're looking for," Joss said, smiling. "Let me know if you need anything else."

As the woman ate, Joss kept an eye on her, noticing that she seemed to be enjoying her pancakes. The diner was busy, but not overwhelming. She knew Dina would be arriving shortly, so she began to pull all the sticky notes down. Joss knew Dina was upset with her for canceling their plans, but she hoped it wouldn't affect their workday.

"That was lovely. Thank you," the woman said, passing her credit card to Joss.

"I'm glad you enjoyed it." Joss smiled, running the card.

"Take ten dollars for yourself. You deserve it."

Going the extra mile was important to Joss. She didn't do things for the extra tip, but it always made a difference for both of the people involved. She only hoped she'd made the woman's day a little brighter.

CHAPTER FOUR

"See you next week," Garth said, waving goodbye.

"I need a vacation like that," Joss said, grinning at Luke.

"Take one." He shrugged. "I'm sure someone could cover for you."

"Maybe someday. Hey, do you mind if I run outside really quickly to make a call?" Joss asked.

"You'll have to ask Dina. I can't go to the tables like this," Luke said, looking down at his shirt.

The minute he'd arrived at the diner for his shift, Luke had spilled French dressing all over himself. He was able to clean up most of it, but it left behind a stain on his white shirt, so going to greet customers wasn't in the cards for him.

"I would, but she doesn't seem to be speaking to me," Joss explained.

"Oh. Uhhh. I mean, should I ask her for you?" Luke asked, looking confused. "Sorry, I just haven't been around adults that aren't speaking in a while. I don't really know how to proceed."

"It's okay. I'll just wait until later."

"Why isn't she speaking to you, and what's with all these pink papers?" Luke said, tossing one into the trash without reading it.

"Sorry. I thought I got them all. She's not speaking to me because I had to cancel some plans we had. I guess the notes are her way of saying things without actually having to talk to me. Honestly, it's been a long time since someone has given me the silent treatment, so I'm not entirely sure what's going on either."

Luke chuckled. "Is it really such a bad thing? I say, as long as it doesn't affect your jobs, just let it go. It should be much quieter around here."

"I'd never dream of letting anything get in the way of my job," Dina said, suddenly appearing out of nowhere. "I have a ton of catering work to do, so I'm gonna go ahead and just take all the tables that come in now, so I can make some cash and Joss can take everything that comes in later. She can take the big party on her own, and I'll help deliver food or whatever."

"Dina. You specifically came in early to help me with the reservation. You basically said that I'd never be able to handle it by myself... according to your note, anyway." Joss crossed her arms. "Why do you get to decide what tables I take?"

"You can do the catering work in between tables or after your shift. You can't just dictate what's going to happen," Luke directed, after Dina hadn't replied to Joss.

"I have so much to take care of for this job, though. It's important," Dina muttered.

"So is your job being a waitress here at the Day and Night Diner. If you can't do both without being fair to your coworkers, then we will reevaluate." Luke glared at Dina.

Joss was quiet, looking back and forth between them.

"It's just that..." Dina began.

"In fact, let's do exactly that. Dina, you go ahead and take some tables while Joss goes over your catering notes. She'll be doing the job. Joss, clock in for catering hours and when you're done, come back out here. I'll call you if it gets busy so that you won't lose out on tips." Luke nodded once and turned on his heel, heading to his office.

Joss was stunned. She knew that Luke would always stick up for her so long as it was deserved, but this was a shock. He was a very lenient boss and business owner, and rarely ever took a stand when it came to how his staff handled things. He always said that so long as they took care of it and the customers were happy, he never minded how things were handled. Clearly, he'd changed his mind.

"Dina. I don't have to do it. I'll go talk to Luke. Or maybe we can both take tables and work on the job together? I'd be more than happy to help," Joss suggested.

Dina pulled out her pack of pink sticky notes and

scribbled something down. She stuck it to Joss's arm and stormed off.

Do it yourself!

Joss stared blankly, watching as Dina left the building. She went into the office to talk to Luke, trying to figure out what her next step should be.

"So that went well," Luke said.

"I don't even want to do the job if it's going to be like this," Joss admitted.

"Too late. I already blocked her from the catering folder on the computer. I changed the password and locked all the paper files in my filing cabinet. If she wants to act like a child, I'll treat her like one." Luke shrugged. "I'll email you the invoice and find out from Dina if there's anything we don't have that's of importance."

"Okay," Joss agreed. "But what about right now? I think Dina actually left."

"Unless you want to call someone in to take her shift, it looks like you're gonna have a busy afternoon," Luke said.

Joss still couldn't believe how Luke was behaving.

Sure, Dina was overreacting and being silly, but Luke never took charge like this. She wasn't sure how she felt about it. For now, though, she'd go over the catering information and see what she needed to do. The diner was still quiet enough where she could take care of her tables at the same time.

She noted that Ryan hadn't come in for the second day in a row and wasn't sure if she should call him or not. She was missing him, but truthfully, she didn't have much time to think about it now. As she went through the email that Luke had sent, she realized just how large of a job the catering event was.

Maybe that vacation she'd mentioned taking earlier wasn't so bad of an idea after all.

CHAPTER FIVE

After a long, hard day at the diner, Joss was finally home. She'd really only been able to skim the information about the catering job while she was at work. When she realized that it was in two days, she found herself a little overwhelmed, but determined to get the job done.

Settling in on her couch, Joss opened her laptop. She had a notebook out and was ready to make a list of everything she needed to do. Thankfully, Dina had already gotten all of the food ordered on a rush delivery, so she didn't have to worry about that part. Joss remembered that after one of their last events, she'd done an inventory of the stockroom and made sure they had everything for the next time around.

Running around at the last minute was never something she liked to do, so it had been her way of making sure it didn't happen, no matter who was doing the catering job.

The event was being held at Natasha Farrell's house, not too far away from her own house. Joss was familiar with the name but only knew Natasha in passing. While Lemon Bay wasn't a big place, it also wasn't one of those *everyone knows everyone else* sort of towns. Natasha and her business partner, Judy, were hosting a party. It wasn't clear what type of event it was, only that it was business-casual, and that the caterer was required to be there the entire evening. Of course, Joss had to work the next morning, but she'd live. Long hours were something she'd become accustomed to over many years in the restaurant industry.

The food was to be prepared at the diner beforehand, and thankfully, the majority of it was pretty easy. She'd be able to get Garth to help her out and would offer him a portion of the tip if there was one. One thing Joss noticed while going over the email was that the bill hadn't been paid in full. Dina's notes showed that Natasha had paid the deposit, and Judy was going to pay the balance before the event. Only, the event was in two days, and no one had come in yet. Joss searched for Natasha's contact information but was unsuccessful. She looked up, down, and sideways for the name of their business as well, also coming up with nothing. Finally, Joss decided to search the Internet, fed up with Dina's lack of details.

Farrell and Faun's Jewelry. Joss knew the women's' names had sounded familiar. She'd purchased a few pieces from them in the past. They did beautiful work. She called the phone number that was listed, hoping to get in touch with someone about the payment. While it wasn't necessarily her responsibility to take care of things like that, she still thought it was better to be safe than sorry. She'd never hear the end of it if she did the job without being paid first, even if it was Dina's fault.

"Hello, Farrell and Faun's," a woman's voice said.

"Hi. This is Josslyn Rockwell with the Day and Night Diner. I'm looking for Natasha."

"She's not available right now. Is there something I can help you with?"

"Maybe. I'm calling about the catering event," Joss said.

"I see. Well, I'm Judy Faun, Natasha's business partner. Perhaps I can answer your questions."

Joss felt comfortable discussing the money situation with Judy since her name was listed on the invoice as well.

"It's about the remaining balance for the event being held tomorrow evening."

"What about it?"

Joss never liked talking about money, even when it related to business. "Well, according to my notes, the balance was to be paid in person at the diner before the event."

"Okay. So, what's the issue?"

"It hasn't been paid," Joss finally said. "The information I have listed stated that Judy Faun will be coming to the diner to pay the remaining balance."

"It says what?!"

Joss was unsure where to go from here. She should have had Luke call, and really wished that Dina had the payment taken care of, but since that wasn't the case, she was on her own.

"I'm sorry. Are you saying the balance won't be paid? I'm going to have to get in touch with my boss, if so."

"No. I apologize. What's the balance? I can drop it off first thing in the morning. Is that too late?"

"I think that will be fine," Joss said. "The balance is $934.18."

"Seriously? I can't believe her."

"Yes, ma'am." Joss cringed.

"Thank you. I'll bring it by in the morning. Is there anyone specific I should ask for?"

"You should be able to drop it off with anyone that's working. Thank you for your help," Joss said, finishing up the phone call.

Before she got a chance to call the diner and talk to Luke about her conversation with Judy and how surprised she seemed to be, she heard a knock on her door. Sighing, she got up, thinking about how nice a few minutes to herself would be.

Joss opened the door. "You're here early!" she said.

"Sorry about that. I got in town ahead of schedule, and thought I'd stop over a little early in case you had any plans for the night," Brandon, her landlord, said.

"Come on in." Joss moved aside. "So, what's the meeting about?"

Things were casual with her landlord. She paid rent early, never asked him for anything unless she couldn't fix it herself. She paid to have her lawn taken care of, her pool, everything. He hadn't raised the rent since she signed the lease seven years previous.

"There have been some changes in my life recently, and it means even more changes are to come. The long and short of it is that I'm going to have to sell the house," Brandon explained, frowning.

Joss needed a moment to process before she spoke. "What does that mean for me?"

"I don't know. I don't even know what it means for me, but you've been a stellar tenant, and I wanted to come to you right away. You deserve to know the truth, so you aren't scrambling to figure things out when the time comes. There's still a lot for me to think about before anything actually happens, but I don't see any other choice. I need the money I'd get from the sale." Brandon finally sat down at the dining room table.

"When? If you sell it, does that mean I have to leave or will whoever buys it continue to rent it to me?" Joss asked, hopeful.

"I can't answer that. Of course, I want you to be able to stay, but after I sell it, it's out of my hands." Brandon lifted his palms as though he was literally letting the house go.

"Okay. Well, ummm. Thanks for letting me know, I guess. I'll start looking for something else. I'd rather not take the chance that whoever buys it will let me stay." Joss wasn't sure if she was sad or frustrated.

"I'm really sorry. Trust me when I say that if I didn't have to do this, I wouldn't." Brandon fidgeted with the placemat.

"I guess it is what it is. These things happen all the time," Joss said.

Brandon sighed. "I'm sorry again, Joss. If I hear of anything, I promise I'll let you know, and I'll give you the best reference I can."

Once Brandon left, Joss briefly considered calling Dina to see if she still wanted to get together, but instead, she turned off all the lights, shut the blinds, and dropped to the couch. It had been a long day, and all she wanted to do was rest.

CHAPTER SIX

Joss knocked on the door three times before someone finally answered.

"Are you with the diner?" the man asked.

"Yes. Josslyn Rockwell." She extended a hand.

"I'm Andy. I live here, but I'm going to stay out of your way. Unless you need help, of course. Do you need help? What am I saying? You're here alone, you're going to need help."

"Wow," Joss said, taken aback by Andy. "I think I'll be okay. I do have quite a few things to carry in, though, so if you have any pets or children, you may want to keep an eye on them while I take care of that. I'll be opening the door several times."

"None of that here." Andy chuckled. "Only me. I'm not a child, but I feel like one. Natasha is on fire tonight. All over the place, dusting things that I don't even think can gather dust. She's been ordering me around all afternoon, so if I accidentally get lost, you know why. Are you sure you don't need any help? Maybe if she sees me helping you, she'll take a few things off my honey-do list."

Joss wasn't sure what to make of Andy. He was undoubtedly very high-strung. She couldn't tell if he was joking or not, but he was definitely making Natasha sound like the queen of tasks. If that was a sign of how the evening would go, she wasn't looking forward to it.

"Joss? I'm Natasha. Don't pay any attention to him. This is our first get together in our new home, and he's just nervous. Feel free to utilize him as you see fit. He's great for carrying in heavy things. The big, strong man that he is." Natasha laughed, patting Andy on the back.

"Okay, sure. I could use a little help," Joss agreed. She figured it'd be easier to just accept the help than keep going back and forth like this, considering she was still standing in the doorway.

"Great! What can I do?" Andy asked.

"Follow me." Joss gestured.

Andy and Joss carried in everything from the catering van. Joss felt bad for Andy and would normally never allow a client to help her set things up, but she made an exception for him. Together, they set up the tables, laid the table runners over the tops, and placed all of the display trays over them. Joss had the food prepared and ready to go and would put it out once it got a bit closer to the actual time of the event.

"What do I do with these? Are they extra?" Andy asked, holding the red linens in his hand, and glancing out the window.

"They can go back in the box. I always bring extra just in case something spills. I hate seeing a messy table runner under all the beautiful food."

"Okay. Well, is there anything else I can do to help? Please," Andy begged. "This was really fun. Much more fun than any project Natasha had for me."

"Not really." Joss laughed. "I just have to bring the boxes back out to the van. Now that they're empty, I'll have no trouble at all handling them."

"How about I do it for you anyway? Maybe you can go chat with Natasha. Calm her down a bit. I know she said I was the nervous one which I am, but this is a pretty big deal for her. It's our new house, and we've got so many people coming, I know she wants to impress them."

"Uhh, okay." Joss nodded. "The van is unlocked, go ahead and put everything in the back. I'll go let Natasha know we're done."

Andy was acting strangely, but then again, he'd been acting that way since she'd arrived. He apparently really wanted to help, so rather than cause any trouble, she just agreed.

"Great," Andy said, picking up a box.

After a half-hour or so, the guests started to arrive. Joss wasn't sure why she had to be there for the entire evening. While there were a lot of guests, there was also a lot of food already out on display. She wasn't sure they'd even go through the first round, never mind need more. No wonder Judy was shocked at the price. Her business partner had spared no expense.

Joss was unfamiliar with most of the people that

were at Natasha and Andy's house. Other than Judy, who she hadn't even really met, Joss was on her own. She did her best to introduce herself to everyone that she could, she also met a few people who were from out of town and loved the food so much they promised to visit the diner the next time they were in the area.

Things were beginning to wind down, and Joss felt like she'd had a great night. Despite the fact that the job was last-minute, and she was basically unprepared, everything went really well.

"Have you seen Andy?" Natasha asked.

"I just saw him a minute ago. He asked if I needed any help, and wouldn't take no for an answer, so I told him he could grab the boxes for me from my van," Joss replied.

"I see." Natasha nodded. "Well, when he comes back can you have him come find me please? I'm going out back for some air."

"Of course," Joss agreed.

Moments later, there was some commotion coming from just outside the front door. Joss ran outside to see if someone was hurt.

She looked around, not seeing anyone.

"Whose house is this and why are you here?!" a woman's voice yelled.

Joss scanned the dark street, looking for people.

"Lower your voice. What are you doing here, Crystal?" Andy asked.

"What am I doing here? What are you doing here? You said you had to be on-site all week for work, and that's why you couldn't be home. But then I find out from my mother, of all people, that you were seen driving around town. So, of course, she followed you here and called me. Don't make me go in there and find out. Whose house is this!?" the woman's voice grew louder, Joss finally realizing they were on the side of the house in the yard.

"It's one of my coworkers. He and his fiancée are having a memorial for her uncle, and I was invited since he worked with us. I didn't plan on coming until he said there wouldn't be many people attending and he felt bad for his fiancée. See, there's basically no one here," Andy said

Joss couldn't believe what she was hearing. Andy was completely lying to whoever the person was that he was talking to. There had been dozens of people there not too long ago. And, to top it all off, he lied and said it was a coworkers house. She knew getting in the middle of whatever was going on probably wasn't smart, but she couldn't just stand there and let him lie.

She cleared her throat, taking a few exaggerated steps across the porch toward the side of the house where the voices were coming from, trying to make herself heard.

"Who's there?! Is that one of your friends?" the woman asked. "Let me go introduce myself."

"No! Let's just get out of here. Come on," Andy said, pulling the woman by the hand through the yard and across the street to a car.

"This is ridiculous. You're lying to me, and I won't stand for it!" the woman yelled.

Andy looked toward the porch, seeing Joss. "I'm not lying to you, but this isn't the time or the place to have that conversation. Let's just go have a nice night somewhere. I'll take you out to eat. Come on, don't cause a scene here. It's a sad time for their family." He opened the car door, letting the woman in, looking at Joss again. This time, his look felt different.

Joss was uncomfortable and raced inside looking for Natasha, wondering if she'd been able to hear what had happened. If Joss could hear it from the front of the house, Natasha would have been able to hear it from the back.

CHAPTER SEVEN

"I can't believe it. What did you say to Natasha?" Tyla asked.

"I didn't. That was the weird part, believe it or not. I think she may have heard the whole thing happen, though. I didn't see her when I got back in the house. There were only two or three people left, one of them her business partner, but she said Natasha came running in the house through the back door with tears in her eyes. Judy said she tried to ask what was wrong but that Natasha just ran upstairs to her room. By the time I left, no one else was there. I didn't even see Judy, but I assume she was upstairs with Natasha by that time."

"Yikes. What a crazy thing to have happened. Who

do you think the other woman was?" Tyla asked, eagerly watching Joss's every move.

"I have no idea." Joss shook her head. "Andy and Natasha were engaged, so it seems weird to think he had a girlfriend."

"Did you tell Judy?"

"No. It's none of my business, really. I'm not even sure what I would have said to Natasha if I had seen her. It's an uncomfortable situation, and it's not like they're my friends. I'm just the hired help."

"I get that, but I'd want to know if it were me." Tyla shrugged.

"Like I said, I'm pretty sure she already knew. Why else would she have run off crying? I mean, this was bad enough, I'm hoping there wasn't something else that upset her that badly."

"True. Either way, I don't envy either of you. I hope she's okay," Tyla said, stacking the last box on the shelf in the stockroom. "I'm gonna go check out front to see if Dina needs anything."

Joss continued organizing the shelves. After a catering

job, everything needed to be put away and invento-ried. She'd verified that everything was good to go so far and only had a couple of boxes left. While she was technically on the schedule for the day, there'd been an accidental over-scheduling, and there were three waitresses there. Joss let Dina and Tyla take care of the dining room while she worked on the project. She was considering asking if she could take the rest of the day off since there was coverage for her to do so.

"Joss," Tyla called. "There's someone here to see you."

"Be right out," she replied, hoping Ryan had come in to see her.

Joss pushed the last of the boxes out of the walkway and got up, brushing herself off. When she came around the corner and looked into the dining room, she saw Ryan. He was sitting at a table and not at his usual stool. A woman was sitting across from him, but before Joss was able to think about it, Verona Price stopped in front of her.

"Verona. Hi. Jeez. I almost ran you down. Excuse me," Joss said, attempting to go around her.

"Actually, I was hoping you had a moment," Verona said, holding up her hand.

"Oh. Yeah, sure. What's up? Was your food okay?" Joss asked, automatically assuming it was related to the diner. Why else would the Chief of Police in Lemon Bay need to talk to her?

"Do you have a place where we could chat?" Verona asked.

"Of course." Joss turned around and led the way to Luke's office.

"Do you have something more private?" Verona asked, looking around the room.

Joss raised a brow. "Sure. Follow me."

When the women arrived in the stockroom, Joss felt like they were hiding out. What could possibly be so important and secretive?

"Perfect. So, I came here because I had a few questions. I knew you'd be working today and felt that you would be cooperative. That's the reason I came here rather than calling you down to the station," Verona said, pulling out a small notebook.

"Calling me down to the station?! What on earth for?" Joss's eyes widened.

"Do you mind telling me where you were last night?" Verona asked.

"At a catering job," Joss said, relieved that she had an answer.

"Can you be more specific?"

"347 High Street. At Natasha Farrell's house. She was hosting a business event." Joss's hands were shaking. She didn't know why she was nervous, but she was.

"What time did you leave?" Verona asked, jotting something down.

"I guess it was a little after ten," Joss replied.

"This isn't a time for guessing." The look on Verona's face was serious.

"I'd say it was somewhere between ten-twenty and ten-thirty, but I wasn't exactly watching the clock. Can I ask what this is about?"

"An open homicide investigation," Verona said matter-of-factly. "How well did you know Natasha Farrell?"

Joss stood still, staring at Verona, but not saying a word.

"Joss. How well did you know Natasha?" Verona asked again.

"Not well. I didn't know her at all, really. Is she... what happened?" Joss asked, leaning against the wall for support.

"Natasha Farrell was found dead in her home this morning. If there is anything you can tell me about last night that might be helpful, now is the time to share." Verona looked up from her notebook, eyes on Joss.

Joss lowered herself to the floor. "I umm. Well... I," she stuttered. "How did she... you know? How did it happen?"

"Is there anything you can tell me about last night?" Verona ignored the question.

Joss certainly hadn't expected the person she'd be explaining the scene between Andy and the other woman to would be Verona. She did her best to recount what she'd heard the evening before. Trying to include everything, even the beginning of the night when Andy had been acting strangely, which could have been a completely normal thing for him. "So, that's it. That's all I know," she finished.

"Sounds like an eventful night." Verona frowned.

"Not really. Not until all that happened. I don't know who the woman with Andy was, and I didn't really get a good look at her either."

"Those were my next questions." Verona nodded. "Thank you for your help. I'll be in touch."

Joss put her hands on the floor, beginning to get up when Verona spoke again.

"Hey, Joss. Do me a favor and stay in town. If you need to leave Lemon Bay for any reason, any reason at all, make sure you contact me first."

Joss lowered herself down again, watching Verona walk away. When she'd first left the stockroom to see who was there for her, she saw Ryan with another woman. She'd thought that was going to be her biggest worry for the day.

CHAPTER EIGHT

"Thanks for coming with me," Joss said.

"That's what friends are for." Tyla grinned. "Plus, I love this kind of thing. Seeing all these different houses is so cool!"

Joss and Tyla pulled into the driveway of the first house on their list. They were going around town looking at the neighborhoods where all of the available houses for rent were to see what Joss thought of them. She knew nothing had happened with her house yet, and she still hadn't heard from Brandon, but this was a great way to get her mind off what had happened to Natasha. She'd gotten a call from Ryan, but just let it go to voicemail. House hunting was her way of ignoring the other parts of her reality.

"Looks like a nice neighborhood," Joss pointed out, taking in all of the well-manicured homes and lawns that lined the street.

"The house is so cute!" Tyla exclaimed, hopping out of the car.

"What are you doing?" Joss asked through the open window.

"Going to look inside. Isn't that what we're here for?" Tyla asked.

"I didn't plan on looking at anything inside. We don't even know if people live here or not. The online listings are wrong sometimes. What if someone already rented it and they're inside while you're peering in their windows?"

"That's crazy. Why would they be listed if someone already moved in?" Tyla marched across the lawn, and onto the porch, cupping her hands to look inside the front window.

"Can I help you?" a woman asked.

Joss jumped in her seat. "I'm so sorry. Do you live here? I knew it! Tyla!"

"I'm Rachel. I just moved in."

"Tyla!" Joss called again. "I'm so sorry. This house was on our list of places that were for rent."

"It's no problem. I hope you find something. I spent forever finding the perfect place."

"Hey! I'm Tyla. Sorry about that. Great house, though." She laughed.

"Are you new in town, Rachel?" Joss asked.

"I am. I've only been here a few weeks. It was nice to meet you both. What did you say your name was again?"

"Sorry again." Joss shook her head. "I'm Josslyn. It was nice to meet you. Welcome to Lemon Bay!"

"We should go," Tyla said out of nowhere.

"I have to get going, anyway. It's almost time for work," Rachel said, waving.

"She seemed nice. Too bad she had a stranger looking in her windows when she came home. How embarrassing!" Joss said, trying not to laugh.

"She did seem nice, but ummm..." Tyla hesitated. "I've seen her before."

"Okay. Where?" Joss asked.

"At the diner yesterday. With Ryan…" Tyla said slowly as though she were afraid to say the words.

"Oh."

Joss didn't know what to say. She and Ryan weren't exclusive, or even official for that matter. She had no right to be upset. After all, Ryan had spent a long time trying to get her to go on a date with him, and she'd said no every time. It wasn't until recently they'd even gone out. If Ryan had somehow met Rachel, even though she was new in town, and asked her out, and she said yes right away, maybe that's what Ryan was looking for. Not to have to chase someone down for a date.

"I'm sorry," Tyla said.

"Don't be." Joss brushed it off. "It's totally fine. Let's go look at the next house, but promise you won't be a peeping tom this time."

"Okay. Let's talk about something else," Tyla said, looking unsure.

"I do have something you might be able to help me with that I've been wondering about…"

"Shoot. What can I do?"

"Find out from Austin how Natasha was killed?" Joss said, putting the car in gear.

"Oh, boy. Just because I'm dating a cop's brother doesn't mean I can just find things out that easily." Tyla tsked. "He probably doesn't even know. It's not like Verona calls Austin to tell him about her homicide investigations."

"True, but you have a better chance at finding out than I do. There haven't really been any details released yet. I think it's all just sort of strange," Joss said, braking at a stop sign and looking at Tyla.

"Strange because you saw Natasha's fiancé arguing with another woman outside and then Natasha was randomly found dead the next morning? Uhh, yeah. I'd say that was pretty strange, too. Not that hard to figure out, though. It seems like a pretty cut and dry case to me."

"So, you think Andy killed her?" Joss asked.

"Andy? Of course not. I think the woman did. Why would Andy do it?"

"I have no idea. Why would Andy have acted like that woman was his girlfriend or something? It was like he was trying to protect her."

"I mean, since he blatantly lied to her about who lived in the house, it's entirely possible there's a lot more going on than anyone knows. But you said you told Verona all about it, so I'm sure she's asking all the right questions to all the right people." Tyla shrugged.

"I guess. I just think that if I can figure out how she was killed, it would help. If Verona has an idea who the killer is, I don't see why she'd have told me not to leave town like I was the one who did it or something. I didn't even know these people."

Joss was torn. She'd just finished saying that she didn't know anyone involved, but she couldn't help but feel like she was involved herself. She'd been there to witness Andy and that woman, and she'd heard that Natasha was upset and in-hiding in her bedroom. Joss should have asked her if she was okay and checked on her before she left. It may not have been her place to do that, but she felt like she was to blame. What if Joss could have stopped Natasha's death from happening at all?

"I'll see what I can find out, but I'm not guaranteeing anything. Austin wouldn't be open about it with me even if he did know something," Tyla admitted.

"You're right. I wonder if we can find out more about Andy. Do you know anything about him at all?" Joss asked, pulling up to the next house on their list.

"No. I never met Andy or Natasha. I'm a little familiar with Judy Faun though, Natasha's partner. She and my mom were friends before my parents moved."

"Maybe you can ask your mom about Judy, then," Joss suggested.

"Why? You think it was Judy now?" Tyla asked.

"I didn't mean that. Just the more information we have, the better, right?"

"This house looks nice," Tyla said, changing the subject.

Joss let it go. She was going to figure out what happened to Natasha one way or another, and if Tyla wanted to help, she was more than willing to let her. All Joss knew was that if she was told not to leave town, it meant something. Something that led her to believe she might be a person of interest in the murder of Natasha Farrell. Whatever it took to make that go away was exactly what Joss was going to do.

CHAPTER NINE

Joss looked at the clock. She didn't think there was a morning that she could remember when Jack hadn't walked in the diner right when the clock hit six a.m. It was unusual for sure, but truth be told, so was everything else in her life. She'd put the house hunting on hold for now, at least until she talked to Brandon again. It's not that Joss had any desire to rush around to look for a place to live because she waited until the last minute, but until she knew for sure what was going on, she decided to push that to the back burner, and take things as they came.

"Sorry I'm late!" Jack called, strolling in the diner, newspaper and umbrella in hand.

Joss smiled. Jack must be in a better mood knowing

that Hazel would be coming back. She hadn't arrived yet that morning either, which was also out of the norm.

"Sorry I'm late!"

This time it was Hazel. She had a huge grin on her face and a gift bag in each hand.

"Good morning to both of you!" Joss greeted two of her favorite customers.

"I have something for you," Hazel passed one of the bags to Joss.

"That's so sweet. You didn't have to do that!" Joss said, turning red.

She loved her customers so much and sometimes felt like they were part of her family. Opening the small, green bag, Joss pulled out a few pieces of tissue paper. Inside was a magnifying glass on the end of a long, silver chain. While it was a beautiful piece of jewelry, Joss didn't understand.

"I was out with my daughter, and we stopped at this little apothecary and trinket type store. I knew I wanted to get you something but was having a hard time finding the perfect thing. The woman who owned the place showed me the necklace, and it was like she knew you personally. The moment I saw it, I knew you had to have it. You're like Lemon Bay's own little detective." Hazel beamed.

Joss laughed. "It's perfect. Thank you."

Hazel gave a slight nod. "I also have something for you," she told Jack.

"Me?" Jack asked, surprised.

Hazel handed the larger of the two bags to Jack, tapping her foot as he slowly reached out to take it from her.

"Go ahead. Open it," she instructed.

Joss watched them, unable to take the smile off of her face. Jack gently pulled out a wrapped box, looking at it for entirely too long.

"I said open it," Hazel demanded.

Jack removed the paper and finally opened the box, peering inside. He placed the box on his table and lifted one side of his jacket, taking out a large envelope.

"This is for you."

Joss felt giddy. She loved romance, and Hazel and Jack were killing her with their interaction. They were the cutest thing ever.

Hazel opened the envelope and burst into a laughing fit. Jack followed her lead. They both laughed and cackled for a few minutes before Joss finally got them to explain.

"What is happening right now?" Joss asked, trying to get a closer look at what they'd given each other. "Are those obituaries?"

Hazel started laughing again, this time holding her side. "What a pair," she said finally.

"You gave her the obituaries?" Joss asked, looking through the newspaper clippings.

"Indeed. I saved them up all week long so she wouldn't miss anything while she was gone." Jack grinned.

"Okayyy. But what's so funny?" Joss still didn't understand.

Jack handed Joss the box he'd received from Hazel. She opened it and stared blankly at what was inside. "You've got to be kidding. You gave him obituaries too?"

"Yup!" Hazel said proudly. "From Charm Hollow. It's where I grew up and where my children live. It's a lovely and eclectic little town just outside of the city. I saved a few of the most interesting ones and packaged them up for a gift."

"Wait. You gave him obituaries from people that he'd never know? What kind of morbid humans are you?!" Joss balked. "And who thinks obituaries are interesting?"

"I think it's great!" Jack said, still chuckling.

"Of course you do." Joss shook her head. "I'm going to start your food. You two crazies enjoy reading about dead people."

Joss still thought Jack and Hazel were sweet, and she was thankful for the gift she'd received from Hazel, but she never understood why people read obituaries for fun.

As Joss buttered a blueberry bagel for Jack and began making Hazel's eggs, she heard her phone ding. After dropping the bagel on the grill, Joss pulled out her phone.

Natasha was found by her cousin in her bedroom closet with a long, red piece of fabric tied around her neck. This message will self-destruct in.... Just kidding, but delete this just in case. I don't want anyone knowing I told you. <3 Tyla

Joss read the message several times before actually deleting it. She tried to remember the night, but as time went on, it became less clear. She wondered if she'd met the cousin. All she could remember was the conversation she'd heard between Andy and that woman. She hadn't thought to look for anyone suspicious during the night. It had to be someone that Natasha knew, though. How else would they be in her bedroom? A thought suddenly crossed Joss' mind. She left the kitchen, running into the stock-room. She frantically pulled open all the boxes until she found what she'd been looking for. Joss counted the red table runners. One was missing. She purposely made sure to bring extra. There'd been six tables set up, and she'd brought eight table runners with her, just in case something spilled. She remembered having that conversation with Andy. She also remembered that Andy was the one to help her set everything up and bring the boxes back in to the van for her. At the end of the night, when she'd been doing the clean-up, things had been awkward, and she just wanted to get out of there. Joss knew all of the guests had gone home, and that Andy had left with the other woman. She hadn't seen Judy, but assumed that she'd gone upstairs to console Natasha. Now, more than ever, Joss had to find a way to talk to Andy. If he had stolen one of the table runners and she could prove it, that could be a really big break in the case. Although, if Verona knew that the table runner belonged to the diner, maybe that was why she was asked not to leave town.

"What's burning? It better not be my eggs! You know I don't like any brown in my eggs!" Hazel yelled.

Hazel was right. Something was burning. Joss ran back to the kitchen only to find everything she'd left on the grill beginning to char. That wasn't the only thing she found, though. Standing next to the grill, just inside the kitchen door, stood Dina, watching the food burn.

"Why didn't you take it off the grill?" Joss asked, throwing everything into the trash.

Dina looked at Joss, looked at the grill, and back to Joss. She shrugged and brushed past her into the office. No doubt to change out of whatever foolish outfit she'd chosen to wear that day.

"Sorry! I'll start fresh!" Joss called from the kitchen, annoyed with Dina. "We don't want to be serving any burnt eggs!"

CHAPTER TEN

"Hey, girl. Do you have a second?" Bridget asked, coming into the diner. "I wanted you to meet my new helper!"

The day had been a long one. Trying to work a busy lunch shift with someone who wasn't speaking to her wasn't Joss' idea of a good time. Twice, Joss had considered calling Becky in early so either she or Dina could go home. She'd finally given up and decided that if Dina didn't want to talk to her, then so be it. She didn't have time to worry about that. A distraction from work was just what Joss needed.

"Sure," Joss agreed, following Bridget out the door.

A woman stood with her back to them, looking at

the cars passing by, multiple dog leashes in her hands.

"Joss this is Rachel," Bridget said, introducing them.

"Hi!" Rachel said, turning around. "Oh. It's you. That was rude. I'm sorry. Hello again."

"You two know each other?" Bridget asked.

"Something like that. Nice to see you again," Joss lied.

Joss thought she was getting a break from things, needless to say, seeing the woman who Ryan was with wasn't exactly what she'd had in mind.

"Rachel just moved to town, and you'll never guess who you two have in common!" Bridget said excitedly.

Rachel and Joss both looked at Bridget, showing signs of confusion.

"Who?" they asked in unison.

"Joss, meet Ryan's sister. Ryan's sister, meet Ryan's lady friend."

"Ryan has a lady friend?" Rachel asked.

"Who says lady friend?" Joss asked.

Joss couldn't believe what she'd just heard. She'd been ignoring Ryan's calls all week for nothing.

"He was on a date with his sister…" Joss mumbled.

"What?!" Rachel laughed.

"I'm so sorry. You must think I'm a lunatic. First, you see me outside of your house, and now this. I'm not sure if I'm Ryan's lady friend as Bridget says, but we've been on a few dates. I didn't even know he had a sister," Joss explained.

"Well, that works out because I didn't know he was seeing anyone."

Joss wasn't offended by that. She hadn't really told many people that she'd been seeing someone either. Probably because it wasn't official, and they'd only been on a few dates. She did feel stupid, though. Thankfully, she'd just ignored Ryan's calls rather than confronting him and embarrassing herself.

"Well, this was nice and awkward. Let's never do it again." Bridget took a few of the leashes from Rachel. "I'll call you later. We gotta go."

"Bye, Joss. Hopefully, we can get together again. I'll let Ryan know I met you," Rachel said.

Joss waved, trying to decide if that was a good sign or not. Rachel seemed nice, but they hadn't exactly met under the best circumstances. She turned back to the diner, hearing a voice call her name.

"You're Josslyn Rockwell, right?" the young woman asked.

"Yes. Can I help you?"

"I'm Marni. I work part-time at Farrell and Faun's Jewelry. I've been meaning to bring you this, but things have just been so crazy lately. I hope you understand."

Joss took the envelope from Marni, having no idea what was inside. She opened it up to find two crisp one-hundred-dollar bills.

"What is this for?" Joss asked, feeling worried. She realized she'd never verified payment after Judy said she'd pay the balance for the catering job. What if that's what this was, and it was still only a partial payment?

"It's your tip. Judy wanted you to have it. She might

have been mad at Natasha for lying, but that wouldn't ever stop her from making sure someone was paid for the work they did. From what I hear, you went above and beyond that night, and she wanted to thank you."

"This is too much." Joss handed it back.

"She said you might say that and told me to tell you to take it anyway."

"Wait. Why was Judy mad at Natasha?" Joss called. "And what did she lie about?"

"I'm sorry. I don't know," Marni said, dashing back to her car.

"Wait!" Joss yelled, going after her.

She was too late. Marni had already reached her car and was halfway out of the parking lot before Joss got close. She pulled her phone out, texting Tyla.

I need to talk to Judy. I'm going today and telling you in case anything happens.

Joss closed her phone and went back into the diner. She hadn't met Marni at Natasha's house that night. If she worked for the company, wouldn't she have been there too? Joss was thankful for the large tip, but cared more about why Judy would have been upset with Natasha. Not like Natasha hadn't had enough to deal with from Andy.

"Dina wants to know why you lied to her." Luke was sitting next to Dina in the office.

"What? Lied about what?" Joss asked.

Luke looked at Dina who proceeded to roll the office chair toward him, whispering her response in Luke's ear.

"She said she knows you were at home and that you could have called her."

Joss knew that Dina was upset about her canceling their plans, but the fact that she knew she was home was too much. Had she been following her?

"How do you know I was home?" Joss asked Dina.

Dina rolled her chair in again, attempting to whisper to Luke. This time Luke backed away, and Dina toppled out of her chair, falling to the floor.

"This is ludicrous. Get yourselves together, ladies. Dina get up off the floor and get to work. If you have something to say to Joss, just say it. And please tell me you weren't following her." Luke shook his head.

"Dina. Seriously. Did you follow me to my house? You can't do that. I'm sorry I bailed on you, and you're right, I was at home. I had a meeting with my landlord, and after he told me he was selling my house, I didn't really feel like hanging out with anyone. Now, if you'll excuse me, I have some side-work to do before I can leave."

Joss pushed past Dina, angrier than she'd been in a while. She knew Dina was an odd duck, and that she didn't have the strongest social skills, but if being stalked was part of being Dina's friend, Joss didn't want to be included.

CHAPTER ELEVEN

"Thanks for meeting with me. I just wanted to stop by and offer my condolences. It's such a shame what happened," Joss told Judy, sitting in the chair across from her at the office space the women used for their jewelry company.

"Thank you. I appreciate that. It's just been such a whirlwind. I never realized there were so many things involved after a business partner passes," Judy admitted.

"I can't imagine. It must be so hard for you."

"To tell you the truth, it's been nice having something to busy myself with. I haven't felt any desire to create any pieces at all lately. Thank goodness for Marni. Natasha didn't let her make many pieces for the company, but the ones she did make were beautiful. I've been selling more of her work after everything that happened, than Natasha's or my own. She's been such a wonderful addition to the team and has been so helpful. Especially now. Such a lovely young woman who is so eager to help. I can't say enough about her."

"Speaking of Marni. She dropped off an envelope to me not too long ago. That was more than generous of you."

"While the event was not quite what I'd expected it to be, that was no fault of yours. It was very well done."

Joss felt her face flush. "Thank you. But I do have to ask. What do you mean it wasn't what you expected? I hope we didn't get anything wrong?!"

"Not at all. I won't trouble you with the messy details." Judy gave a small smile.

Judy had no idea that Joss knew anything about Andy, and Joss had no idea if Judy knew either. Rather than letting the conversation go in circles, Joss made an attempt to switch things up.

"I don't mind listening if you need someone to talk

to," Joss offered, prepared to admit the truth, but hoping Judy would be the one to say it first.

"The food and service were great, dear. Natasha did a lovely job choosing you. I just wish she'd been honest with me about why we were all there. She had to have realized that I'd catch on sooner or later."

"I'm not following," Joss said, feeling like this wasn't about Andy.

"Natasha was a very intelligent woman. She was excellent at creating jewelry. She had an eye for it. She was one of the savviest businesswomen I'd ever encountered in all of my fifty-something years. Her one fault was mixing business with pleasure. I can't even fault her for that, actually, I take that back. Natasha's ability to network was second to none. There were several occasions when she'd have a plan in mind, and invite everyone she knew in her personal life, and suddenly we had twenty new clients. Let's just say she'd been known to be clever in her business practices." Judy sat back and crossed her legs.

Joss, thinking on her feet, quickly replied, "That must have made for an interesting partnership, but as you said, you gained clients every time, so it can't be all bad."

"Interesting." Judy chuckled. "You can definitely call it that."

"Normally, I wouldn't be so nosy, but I wanted to ask. How is Natasha's fiancé dealing with everything?" Joss purposely left out the fact that she remembered Andy's name just fine.

"I wouldn't have any idea about Andy." Judy's detest for the man was evident.

"My apologies. I didn't know. I just assu..."

"There's no way you could. Andy wasn't my favorite person, and Natasha knew that. Heck, some of her closest family members felt the same way about him, so she never told us a thing. Of course, things didn't start out that way." Judy looked away, as if remembering something specific.

"Do you happen to know where Andy is staying or maybe even where he works? I'd love to send him something, a casserole, even a sympathy card."

"Beats me. I attempted to send something as well,

thinking it would be a kind gesture, even though we weren't always on the best of terms."

"Attempted?" Joss asked.

"I didn't know where Andy was staying, but I knew he worked at Cartwright Construction. He was an architect and traveled a lot working on some high-profile jobs. That's why the night was such a big deal for Natasha, I think. He hadn't been around in weeks. I had some flowers sent, which in retrospect, probably wasn't the best choice, but the flower shop called me to let me know that there was no one that worked there by that name, and the delivery had been refused. Of course, I called the company right away. I was so upset about it. Come to find out, Andy never worked there at all. They'd never even heard of him. So yes, I attempted to be kind and show my sympathy for the man my business partner and best friend was engaged to, but some things never change. Andy has been lying to Natasha for a long time, and I always just looked past it. If I were you, I'd stay away. I know you mean well, but seeking out a man like that may not be in your best interest." Judy spoke clearly, emphasizing the last few sentences.

Joss wasn't surprised to hear that. No matter how much she wanted to see the good in people, sometimes it just wasn't there. Not only had Andy lied to that woman on the night of the catering event about where they were, but he also lied to Natasha about where he worked. If that was the case, it was probable that he'd lied about plenty of other things.

"That's quite a lot to handle. I think I'll take your advice and stay away. I appreciate you being so honest with me," Joss said. "You didn't have to do that."

"It may be a farfetched thought, but if you took the time to extend that man kindness, I wouldn't put it past him to make a move on you. I'm sure it wouldn't be the first time."

"What? He didn't... I would never." Joss was surprised.

"I didn't mean with you. I mean with Natasha's cousin. Gloria was the only person I knew that stood up to him and Natasha both. She tried her best to keep them apart, but Natasha believed Gloria wanted him for herself. It's all a big mess, really. And I've bored you long enough. I'm sorry for unloading all of this on you, but I just wanted you to be cautious around Andy. He's not who he portrays himself to be."

"Of course. It's no trouble at all. I'm glad you told me," Joss said, rising from her seat. "Thanks again for your honesty and the generous tip. It was much more than necessary."

"Like I said. You deserved it. You'd never have gotten a thing if we left it up to Natasha. She liked to spend money... just in all the wrong places." Judy stood, walking Joss out of the office.

CHAPTER TWELVE

"So, I hear you met my sister," Ryan said, sitting on the fourth stool from the register, his designated favorite spot.

"I did." Joss nodded, hoping Rachel had spared him the details.

"She said you were looking for a new place to live. How come I had to find that out from my sister?" Ryan asked, looking concerned.

Joss breathed a sigh of relief. She was glad that was what Ryan had chosen to focus on. Not that Tyla had been peering in her windows, or that Joss had said something about Rachel dating her brother.

"I found out that my landlord is selling the house. I

don't need to leave yet or anything, but I'm pretty sure it's not too far off," Joss explained.

"Can he do that? Have you looked over your lease?" Ryan asked.

"No." Joss shook her head. "But I'm not going to try to fight it or anything. He came to me right away. Nothing has even happened yet."

Ryan looked skeptical. "Are you sure? It's possible that there may be something in the lease that can protect you."

"I'm okay." Joss laughed. "I don't need protection. I just need a new place to live. I've lived there for a long time. Maybe a change will do me good."

"If you say so," Ryan replied, still looking unsure. "What else have you been up to? I tried calling you a few times, but it just kept going to voicemail."

"About that...." Joss began. She wanted to be honest with Ryan, no matter how embarrassing. "I was in the back working the other day when Tyla came to tell me someone was here to see me. My first thought was you, and while you were here, you were also here with another woman. I might have misunderstood things a little."

When Ryan finally finished laughing, he spoke. "You thought... You thought I brought another woman to the diner and requested to see you? What kind of person would do that? I did bring her in to meet you, but she's just my sister."

"I know that now, but I was distracted when it wasn't you at all that wanted to see me. It was Verona."

"Oh, boy. You in trouble with the law?" Ryan teased.

"I don't know anymore. I haven't heard from her since, but nothing seems to have changed, so I'm not really sure where I stand." Joss shrugged.

"Wait. I was kidding. What are you talking about?"

After explaining everything that had happened to Ryan, Joss had to walk away to take care of her other customers. The diner wasn't terribly busy, and Dina was there working as well, but she still wasn't speaking to Joss, so Joss had to make sure to keep an even closer watch on her tables. Normally, they all looked out for one another at the diner, but things with Dina were still awkward. Thankfully, Ryan was the only one at the counter, and the rest of the customers were in the larger section of the diner, not near where Ryan and Joss were talking, giving them a little more privacy.

"Have you been sitting there with your mouth open the entire time?" Joss asked when she'd finally made her way back to Ryan.

"I'm a little surprised is all. Are you okay? Have you been...trying to, ya know?" Ryan asked, cryptically.

"To what? Solve the murder?" Joss asked, grinning. "I'm an interested party who heard a few things that I wasn't supposed to hear. You'll be happy to know that I was going to try to find Andy, but was able to find out some things about him before I had the chance. After that, I decided it was better for my safety that I didn't try to find him.

"Let me make sure I get this right. I'm supposed to be happy that you didn't see him because if you did, it might have been dangerous?" Ryan asked.

"Sounds about right." Joss laughed, refilling Ryan's root beer.

"I'm glad you didn't get to go. I don't think you should be purposely putting yourself in danger."

"I didn't purposely do anything. I had no idea that

this guy was as bad as Judy claimed he was. In fact, I still don't even know if she was telling the truth or exaggerating or what. All I know is that she said that Andy was a liar and that I should stay away from him. I also know she gave me a two hundred dollar tip."

"Dang! You taking me out on a date?" Ryan joked, his eyes twinkling.

"I'm giving half to Garth for helping me with all the food," Joss said, rolling her eyes. "A hundred dollars can still go a long way, though. We really should do something again soon."

"We should." Ryan nodded. "And we will. How about we go to an amusement park this weekend? I hear one opened up not too far away from here. A couple of hours, but that's not too bad."

"I haven't been to one of those in years! What's it called? I'll have to check it out online. I gotta see what rides they have so I can prepare myself for scary roller coasters before we go. I'll also be researching all of the midway games if they have any. I like to think of myself as a professional whack-a-mole and ski-ball player."

"Of course you do. Game on, by the way. I'm the ski-ball champion," Ryan boasted. "It's Jamboree Junction. You may remember it as Riverside Park though, it was closed down and abandoned for years, but I heard that whoever bought it really fixed the place up nice. So, it's a date?"

"It's a date." Joss grinned, excited to talk to Ryan again. She felt a little foolish for ignoring his calls and assuming the worst when it really hadn't been anything bad at all.

"Hey." Ryan pointed. "Is that the older couple you talk about all the time?"

Joss looked out the window. Jack, Hazel, a second older man, and a woman about her age were all on their way into the diner.

"Yes. It's weird to see them here so late in the day, though, and together, for that matter," Joss mused. "This oughta be interesting."

CHAPTER THIRTEEN

"Look who's here!" Joss exclaimed, greeting Jack and Hazel at the door.

"We weren't going to come here at first, but when we ran into Hazel, she insisted," Jack said.

"I'm glad you changed your mind." Joss smiled, gesturing for the group to have a seat.

"They were about to go to some restaurant in the city, but I saw them at the gas station and suggested they come here instead. I thought it was a much better option," Hazel said, still standing.

"Well, sit, why don't ya?" Jack looked toward Hazel.

"No, no. This isn't my meal," Hazel said, holding up her hands.

"Nonsense. Tell me you didn't just follow us here to make sure we arrived safely. Sit down and eat with us," Jack said again.

Joss watched the older man and younger woman that had come along. They were looking back and forth at Jack and Hazel as though they were watching a tennis match.

"Do they do this often?" the man asked.

"Oddly enough, yes." Joss nodded. "But it's all in good fun. I think..."

"Ernie, Gloria, this is Joss. My favorite waitress," Jack introduced his friends, still waiting for Hazel to sit.

"Nice to you meet you both," Joss said. "Are you from around here?"

"We live in the city. We had a family member pass away, and we had some things to take care of here," Gloria explained.

It took Joss' mind a moment to register, but the second it did, she gave Hazel a look.

"I'm sorry for your loss. Are you here for Natasha Farrell by any chance?" Joss asked.

"Yes. That's right. I'm her cousin, and this is our grandfather. Did you know her?" Gloria asked, nudging Ernie.

Joss gave a brief explanation, not wanting to impose on their lunch.

"On that note. I'm going to head out," Hazel said, winking at Joss. "Enjoy your meals."

"She sure is an interesting woman," Ernie pointed out.

Jack nodded.

"Well, can I get you all anything to drink while you look over the menu?" Joss asked, her mind spinning. It wasn't hard to figure out that this was Natasha's family. Tyla had said Natasha's cousin found her and Judy mentioned the name, Gloria. She wondered how Hazel knew that Joss would want to talk to them, it was like that woman had a sixth sense about things sometimes.

The group ordered their drinks and food at the same time, making the process much quicker. All Joss could think about was getting a chance to talk to Gloria. It seemed that Ernie was rushing everyone along, as though he didn't want to be there for any longer than he had to.

After delivering their food, Joss left them alone, glancing over to see if she could catch Gloria's eye. At one point, she raised her hand, calling Joss over.

"Can we get the check please?" she asked.

"I'm not even done eating yet," Ernie said.

"Where's the race?" Jack asked, chuckling. "You that eager to get back to the city traffic?"

"Very funny," Gloria grumbled. "I remembered I have an appointment this evening and can't be late. We should get going, Grandad."

The group finished up their meals, taking the left-overs in to-go boxes. Ernie paid the bill and Gloria ushered him out of the diner.

"Is she always like that, or did I do something wrong?" Joss asked Jack.

"I think it's hard for them to be here is all. When you mentioned knowing Natasha, it may have been too much. I believe they were a really close family."

Before Joss got the chance to reply, Gloria came running back into the diner.

"Quick, I told my grandfather I needed to use the restroom before we made the trip back home. I just had to ask you something before we left."

"Okay." Joss nodded, wondering why she was in such a rush.

Jack stepped away to give them some privacy, looking at the wall décor as though it was his first time seeing it.

"You were there the night she was killed," Gloria stated.

Joss frowned. "I was catering an event at her home, yes."

"Did you notice anything strange?" Gloria asked. "Everyone we ask that was there says everything seemed normal as ever. But you being an outsider may make a difference."

"I mean, I wasn't really looking for anything out of the ordinary. I think Natasha and her fiancé may have had something going on," Joss began.

"See? I knew that jerk had something to do with it!"

Gloria said. "Did he say anything to you?"

Joss sighed. She was afraid to explain what had happened, but finally decided it was best her family knew. After telling Gloria what had happened between Andy and that woman, Joss noticed Jack heading outside to Ernie's car.

"I'd been warning Natasha to stay away from him since the beginning. I had a gut feeling he was lying to her, and apparently, I was right."

"Didn't she believe you?" Joss asked.

"No," Gloria said, shuffling her feet. "Unfortunately, Natasha and I weren't on great terms. She always refused advice from me because of something that happened back when we were in college. We were both interested in the same man and when I won, so to speak, she told everyone that I stole him from her. Ever since then, she refuses to listen to anything I say. For crying out loud, Andy was about the sketchiest man I'd ever encountered, and the only thing Natasha could think about was how I was feeding her bad information about him so I could have him for myself."

"I had no idea. He seemed so nice at first, but when I

heard him outside, I just wasn't sure what to do. Is all of what you just mentioned the reason you weren't at the party?" Joss asked.

"She invited me, actually. Which I'd say was a surprise, but she always invited me to business events because I work in marketing and advertising. She knew having me around was good for business, if it was a personal event, she'd have never invited me." Gloria glanced out the window. "I'd better get going. Here's my card. Give me a call. We should get together again and talk more. I'd love to nail Andy to the wall. He's a fast talker and great at distracting people, so they don't think anything of his scams. If you see him, watch out," she said, rushing back outside.

Joss thought back to when she'd talked to Judy. She had gotten the feeling that Natasha used business money for personal events but still called them business events to cover up where the money was going. Maybe Judy was wrong. Gloria had just said that Natasha would have never invited her to a personal event. Hopefully, Judy didn't have the wrong information, because spending shared business money on a personal event was certainly a solid reason for Judy to be upset.

CHAPTER FOURTEEN

Scooping up the last bit of rolled silverware, Joss carried it over to the bucket where Dina was sitting in the reservation room used for large parties, rolling her own silverware for her after shift side-work. She sat there at the table with Dina for a few moments trying to decide if it was worth trying to make conversation again. There was only so many times that Joss would make an effort before giving up. Chasing people wasn't something she was interested in doing.

The decision was made for her when her phone started ringing. Not missing the serious eye roll that came from Dina, Joss answered, seeing Tyla's name on the caller-id.

"Hello."

"You are never going to believe what just happened! I'm at the barber with Austin. I tricked him into taking me with him, so I could go shopping in the little shops near where he goes while he was getting his hair cut. Apparently, a lot of the cool shops that used to be here, aren't here anymore, so I just went back and sat at the barbershop. I wasn't there five minutes when a woman came in looking for a guy named Andy. The owner of the place said he was out due to a death in the family and wouldn't be back until next week."

"Andy?" Joss guessed. "This is great! Now we know where he works and that he for sure lied about being an architect. What did the woman say? Do you think it was the same one from that night?"

"It was weird because she seemed shocked to find out that he even worked here. She said she hadn't seen him in days and knew it was the time he told her he went for his cut and shave every week, so she decided to stop in, hoping he'd be there."

"Is she still there?" Joss asked.

"Not at the barber, but I'm outside talking to you, and I saw her go into a fast-food place across the plaza."

"Did you catch her name? Actually, never mind. Can you do me a favor? It's kind of crazy."

"I didn't hear her name. What do you need me to do?"

"Can you get a picture of her? Like, go over by the restaurant or her car or something and try to secretly snap a picture? I didn't see the woman the night of the event very well, but if I saw her again, it might help. It might not even be the same person, knowing how friendly Andy seems to be with the ladies, so if you can't do it, it's totally fine.

"I'm on my way. I'll call you back."

Joss heard silence on the other end of the line. Tyla had already hung up and was likely trying her best to stealthily make her way over to where the other woman was, all while trying to keep Austin from paying attention to what she was doing. Joss knew her best friend all too well.

"Hey, ladies," Garth said, coming around the corner from the kitchen.

"I thought you were on vacation?" Dina asked, looking surprised.

"I am." Garth nodded. "I only came to pick up my paycheck. You wouldn't have to twist my arm too hard to get me to work, though. Vacations aren't all they're cracked up to be. I've been bored since it started."

"I have something that might help!" Joss exclaimed, hopping up and going to the office. "Here. Now you can go do something fun and enjoy your vacation a little more with this unexpected cash!"

"What is this for?" Garth asked, pulling out a one-hundred-dollar bill from the envelope.

Dina eyed Joss, clearly eager for an answer as well.

"It's the tip from that catering job," Joss explained.

"Dang. I don't have any change to break it in half, does the register?" Garth asked, pulling out his wallet.

"It's yours," Joss said.

"All of it?" Garth was surprised.

"I told you I'd split the tip if we got one since you helped me out so much."

"Must be nice," Dina said, looking at Garth.

Ignoring her, Garth spoke, "I thought the event didn't go well. I'm surprised we got anything at all."

"The event went great. It was what happened afterward that was the problem. It was actually a few days later when I got this. Judy, the business partner of the woman that was killed, sent one of their employees here to give it to me. I was surprised, too. Who would have thought that a little event for a small business would have earned us such a great tip?!"

"This is great. I'm glad I stopped by. Now, I can pay my bills and still do something fun. It's my lucky day!" Garth chuckled.

"Me, too! Let's do it again sometime. Minus the murder, of course." Joss laughed, passing Garth his paycheck from under the cash register drawer.

"Thanks, Joss. And thanks to you too Dina for deciding not to do the event. I'd never have gotten this," Garth said, waving the cash.

"I didn't *decide* anything. And don't act like I wouldn't have shared the tip." Dina dropped her silverware in the bucket and left the room.

"She's a real peach, huh?" Garth mused, watching

Dina stomp off. "She'd never have shared the tip either, by the way."

"She's mad at me and acting like a child. One of these days, it's going to come back and bite her. She's going to have no choice but to talk to me."

"Have fun with all that," Garth said, getting ready to leave. "I'm going to hit some golf balls with my extra money. See ya later."

Since her side-work was complete, Joss clocked out of work and pulled out her phone. She'd been waiting to hear back from Tyla, but while she was busy chatting with Garth, she'd missed a call and a text from her. Opening the text, Joss couldn't help but be simultaneously entertained at Tyla's craziness and thrilled with what she saw.

"I don't have a picture to send you. I'm sorry. But what I do have is information. I was trying hard to be sneaky, and it was an epic fail. She totally caught me trying to take her picture, and it was super awkward. Anyway, her name is Crystal, she's Andy's wife, and she wants to meet with you privately. She said PRIVATELY! I'm going with you, though, because if she's a killer, I'll feel terrible sending you on your own. Call me when you get this. We'll go today."

Andy was married to Crystal and engaged to Natasha. He lied about where he worked and lived, and no one in Natasha's inner circle seemed to like him. He certainly had the jerk factor going for him, but he had a wife and a fiancée... if that wasn't a motive for murder for Crystal, then Joss didn't know what was.

CHAPTER FIFTEEN

"Are you sure this is a good idea?" Joss asked, feeling anxious.

"Aren't you supposed to be the murder solver here? It'll be okay. We're in a public place, and I'll be nearby. I'm wearing a disguise, see." Tyla held up her hat and glasses.

"Great disguise." Joss rolled her eyes. "Make sure you sit with your back to her."

Joss and Tyla had arrived thirty-minutes early to the coffee shop where Crystal had agreed to meet. They wanted to make sure that they were there before her so they could get their seats so Tyla would be able to sit close enough to overhear, but not be recognized.

"I'll be right back. I'm gonna order a coffee so I'm

ready. I'll be nice and caffeinated in case we need to chase her or something. How fun would that be?" Tyla squealed.

"A blast." Joss rolled her eyes again, settling in and making sure Tyla's jacket was draped over the booth behind her to save her seat.

"Okay, I'm ready. Do you know what you are going to say to her?" Tyla asked. "Helloooo. Why aren't you answering me?"

"Crystal?" Joss said, loud enough to shut Tyla up.

"I remember you," Crystal said, sitting down across from Joss. "From the diner."

"That's right. I remember you too. You seemed to be upset that day."

"I was. And I suppose this is how the world works, too. It all comes together, doesn't it? When you saw me that day, I hadn't said more than two words to my husband in four days. I'd call him, and every time he'd claim he was busy with work, or on a construction site and couldn't talk. I was sick and tired of the way things were going, and I still am. While showing my feelings in public isn't some- thing I typically like to do, I'm sort of glad that I did.

Now, here we are," Crystal said, picking up her menu.

"Excuse me, but I'm just going to be blunt. I don't think we are going to get anywhere beating around the bush. Is Andy really your husband?" Joss asked.

"We are still legally married, yes. We've been separated for some time now, but we were working things out. Or, at least we were supposed to be."

Joss moved around in her seat, hoping the next few minutes weren't going to be as awkward as she expected them to be.

"My friend Tyla, the one you met at the barbershop..." Joss began.

"Yes. Let's get it all out of the way," Crystal said. "I went to see him there because it was his normal weekly appointment time. I guess that really wasn't the truth, though. You can't imagine how I felt when I walked in there, after not seeing him for days, only to find out that he doesn't just get his hair cut there, he works there."

"Does he not really work in construction?" Joss asked.

"Beats me. I don't know much of anything anymore. He lied about where he worked, and he lied about where he lived. He lied about everything." Crystal tossed the menu down.

Joss took a deep breath, realizing she'd just had the same thoughts herself about all of Andy's lies. "I saw you talking to him."

"I know. Your friend told me. You could have said something. Told me the truth or something."

"And say what? I didn't know who you were or why you were there. I don't even know Andy or Natasha either," Joss explained.

Crystal froze. "Don't mention her name again."

"Okay." Joss nodded. "I won't. Have you seen Andy at all?"

"Why? You just finished saying you didn't know him. Why does it matter?" Crystal asked. "Unless you were seeing him too, and if that's the case, then this conversation is going to go an entirely different way."

Joss sighed. "Of course I wasn't seeing him."

"Wasn't? So, does that mean you weren't then but were at one point?" Crystal raised her voice.

Joss's phone buzzed. She picked it up, glancing at the text message from Tyla. *Jealous much?*

"I never dated him. I never had feelings for him. In fact, I'd never even met him until that night. You seem to think that Andy saw several women on the side. Is that true?"

"I wouldn't put it past him. But to answer your question, no, I haven't seen him. Not since the night that...wretch...got herself killed. As you know, Andy and I left together. We went back to our...my house and talked for hours. Until now, I'd have stuck up for him and lied for him until I turned blue in the face, but now that I have to talk to strangers about our relationship, I give up. I'm not going to be embarrassed anymore. Andy didn't stay at my house all night. We talked and then he left. He said that it would make things confusing if he stayed over, so he left, saying he was going to get a hotel room."

"Did you believe him?" Joss asked.

"I mean, I guess. I'm not sure why since I apparently can't trust him at all anymore, but at the time, I saw no reason to think that he wasn't actually going to a hotel."

Joss nodded. "And you haven't heard from him since? Don't you think that's a little strange?"

"Yes. I do. That's why I'm here. I'm not done with him yet. He needs to know how he made me feel. Your friend told me you liked to find details related to things like this, and I wanted to meet with you so we could talk. I thought maybe you could provide me with some information about where he is."

"I'm sorry. I don't have any answers for you," Joss said.

"I knew this would be a waste of time." Crystal waved a hand to call over the waitress. "I'm ordering food, so it's not a totally wasted trip."

"Listen," Joss whispered. "Just because I don't know where your husband is, doesn't mean you get to be rude. You asked to meet me, not the other way around. I came here to find out if Andy killed Natasha." She enunciated her name and drew it out as long as she could knowing Crystal wouldn't like it.

The waitress came over, and Joss apologized, telling her they needed a few more minutes.

"Andy?" Crystal scoffed. "You came here to ask me if I thought Andy killed someone? The same Andy who screamed when he saw a bug? The one who was afraid to be outside alone at night? Please, I always had to do the dirty work for him, because he was anxious over everything. He may have been a liar, a fast-talker, and a cheater, but he couldn't have killed someone."

Joss could agree that Andy seemed anxious, but one thing that wasn't adding up was that he didn't like to be outside alone at night. If Crystal was telling the truth, then why did Andy offer to carry out the boxes at night by himself from the catering event?

"He was outside alone on the night I saw you and him talking," Joss pointed out, hoping for an honest answer.

"I suppose that's true. But he was a bumbling fool too. Seconds before he realized I was there, he dropped whatever he was carrying, the contents spilling out all over the porch and down the stairs. It couldn't have been me that surprised him because he hadn't even seen me yet. I stand by what I said. Andy couldn't have killed her. He didn't have it in him." Crystal raised a hand calling over the waitress again.

Andy dropped the box he'd been carrying which

was likely the noise that Joss had heard right before she'd gone outside to check on things. The only thing in those boxes other than a couple of extra display trays and some utensils were the extra table runners. The red linen cloth that was wrapped around Natasha's neck. That gave both Crystal and Andy, and anyone who was left at the house that night a prime means of killing Natasha. If Andy dropped a table runner, and then was distracted by seeing Crystal, anyone there could have picked it up and used it to kill Natasha. Joss needed to find out who had access to the house and the time of her death. Crystal said Andy left in the middle of the night, and he had access to the house, but no real motive. Crystal didn't have easy access to the house, but it wasn't impossible, and she definitely had motive. Judy had the motive and opportunity, and from what Joss knew, was still inside the house when she'd left for the night. This wasn't getting any easier. They needed to get out of there and talk. Joss needed Tyla to get information from Austin or Verona.

"Thank you for your time. I'm glad we met, but I have to be going. If you hear anything from Andy, please let me know." Joss took a few bills from her purse, placing them on the table. "Your meal is on me."

Crystal looked up at Joss. "I'd say for you to call me if you heard from him too, but I think if I saw him right now, I'd ring his scrawny little neck."

CHAPTER SIXTEEN

"What's going on? You're here for the second time in a week after your normal time. Are you playing tricks on me?" Joss joked.

"I'm glad you're here. I was hoping we could talk for a few minutes," Jack said. "Are you busy right now?"

"If you give me a few minutes, I can step outside. Is everything okay?"

"I'll let you decide that. I'll be outside."

Joss checked on her tables and asked Luke to ask Dina to watch them while she was gone because, of course, Dina still wasn't speaking to her.

"What's going on? Are you alright?" Joss asked again.

"I'm doing just fine. Do you remember the people I came in here with the other day?" Jack asked.

Joss nodded.

"Well, Ernie and I have been friends for years, and he's worried about his granddaughter. He claims she's been acting strangely, has taken all this time off from work, but spends all her time in her office alone. He's worried that she's not handling things well."

"I'm sorry to hear that, but I'm not sure why you're telling me."

"Ernie has tried to go to Gloria's office several times, and she won't let him in. I know this isn't in your job description as a waitress, but I thought maybe you could check on her or something. You two are about the same age, and you are always so easy to talk to. Then there's that whole thing with you solving crime. You're right. It's a bad idea, forget I even mentioned anything." Jack began to walk away, not even letting her speak.

"Not on your life, mister. I can definitely check on her. Do you have her address?"

"I don't. All I know is that she works for herself and has a little office somewhere in the city." Jack frowned.

"Wait!" Joss exclaimed. "When you were here before, she gave me her business card. I'm sure it's on there. I'll give her a call or maybe stop by to see if I can help. I'm not sure what I'll really be able to do. You aren't thinking she killed her cousin or anything, are you? I don't want to be purposely walking into a bad situation."

"I don't think it's that serious. I just think she needs someone to talk to. Normally, from what Ernie says, she's full of life and always there to help him with things he can't handle on his own. I just get the feeling that something isn't right."

"Of course. I'll do everything I can," Joss agreed, feeling bad. She didn't think there was anything she could do to make a person feel better after losing a family member. It wasn't just not in her job description, it was something she'd never had to do before, but when someone asked her for help, she always had a hard time declining.

———

Joss had called Tyla, Bridget, Ryan, and even considered asking Dina to come with her to see Gloria.
Honestly, if Dina hadn't been the only one working
at the diner, she may have asked her even though
Dina still wasn't speaking to her. No one was
answering her calls, so that meant she'd have to go
on her own. Joss plugged in the address from the
business card that Gloria had given her and drove
the forty-minutes to the city.

When Joss pulled into the parking lot, she was
surprised. The small building stood on its own, with
nothing on either side of it. Gloria must be doing
well with her business to have such a great office
space that she wasn't sharing with anyone. She
looked around, not seeing any other vehicles nearby,
assuming that Gloria wasn't there. Figuring she'd
give it a shot anyway; Joss got out of her car and went
to the front door of the building.

"Knock, knock," she said, trying the door. "Is anyone
here?"

Hearing nothing, she put her hands to the door to
block the light and peered inside. At first, the only
thing she saw was a loveseat and a couple of chairs
in what looked to be the waiting room. Out of the

corner of her eye, she swore she saw movement. Her heart racing, she blinked a few times and looked again. Beginning to laugh, Joss shook her head. She'd seen movement alright, but it was just herself that she saw. There was a mirror in the room, where she could see her reflection. She'd been scared for no reason. Walking around the side of the building to see if there was more parking in the back, where Gloria's vehicle may be, Joss saw a window. She usually wasn't much of a snooper, but this time, things got the better of her. Not tall enough to see inside, she rolled a large rock that was near the door over toward the window and looked around, making sure no one was nearby. She stepped on the rock and looked through the window. While she couldn't see much through the slats of the blinds, what she could see knocked her right off the rock.

Acting faster than she was able to think, Joss picked up the rock and threw at the window, hoping it would break. She hadn't considered that there would be an alarm and was thankful when there wasn't.

"Mmmm... Mmmppffh..." Andy tried talking through the tape over his mouth.

Joss took off her shoe, running it along the window to knock out the rest of the broken glass. She stepped back and took a running leap, grabbing on to the window and somehow wriggling herself inside, and taking the tape from Andy's mouth.

"Oh, my gosh. Are you okay? What happened? Where is Gloria?"

"Not here. She went to get me something to eat. She's only been feeding me once a day. We need to get out of here. Now! That woman is insane!"

"How long has she been holding you here?" Joss asked, freeing Andy's hands.

"Since the day Natasha was found. She thinks I killed her and now she wants to kill me. She's been telling me about all the ways she can think of to kill me, and how to make a clean getaway. She just sits here on her computer all day, reading to me from the internet all the different ways people can be killed," Andy said, ripping the ropes from his legs. "I'm telling you, she's crazy, and we need to get out of here. Let's go out the front before she comes back. She always comes through the back door, so if we're quick, she won't see us or notice the broken window right away."

Andy and Joss ran to her car, getting in and peeling out of the parking lot, putting their seatbelts on as they went.

"We have to go to the police!" Joss said, making a turn.

"Can't we go back to Lemon Bay? I want to get as far away as possible from here. Please," Andy begged.

"Fine, but we're going right to the police station when we get back. Or the hospital, you need to get checked out," Joss said, eyeing the cuts on Andy's face.

"I can't believe this. The love of my life is killed, and I get kidnapped by her crazed cousin."

"The love of your life? You obviously aren't talking about your wife," Joss asked without thinking.

"Ouch." Andy nodded, rubbing his wrists. "I know I'm a bad guy. I like women. I don't make good choices. You don't need to remind me."

"You're right." Joss felt bad for the guy. "You really think Gloria killed Natasha?"

"It wasn't the first person on my mind, but after this, it's hard to deny it."

"Who was the first person on your list?" Joss asked, thinking of Crystal.

"Judy Faun. Natasha's business partner. The night of the party, after well, you know... I went to Crystal's house to talk. We are separated, but she deserved an explanation. Once I was done there, I went back home to Natasha who also deserved an explanation, because I know she saw me leave with Crystal. I saw her watching us as we drove away and I never should have left. When I got back to the house, I saw Judy's car still there. I didn't want to try talking to Natasha with Judy there, so I just left. I went and got a room at Lemon Bay Hotel."

"Why couldn't Judy have been there as a friend, sitting with Natasha after you took off?"

"I'm not sure I'd call them friends. Judy barely tolerated Natasha. They ran their business like champions, but what went on behind closed doors was a whole other story."

The two drove in silence the rest of the way. Joss hadn't replied to Andy, and it was clear Andy was tired, and stressed out and just wanted to relish in his freedom.

"We're here," Joss said, pulling into the police station. "Come on."

CHAPTER SEVENTEEN

Joss had heard through the grapevine that Gloria had been found and brought in for the murder of her cousin Natasha Farrell. It turned out that no matter what Andy or anyone else thought, the police had everything taken care of. Verona was annoyed, but thankful that Joss had found Andy and brought him in to talk to her.

Luke had given Joss the day off, joking that she deserved it for all the pain and suffering that the catering event had caused her. Her plans were to meet up with Ryan later in the day and talk over dinner about their trip to Jamboree Junction. It had been a long time since Joss had an entire day off with nothing to do, so she decided to go check out the animals at the shelter at the request of Bridget. Even if she didn't adopt an animal, she thought that maybe she could visit and play with them for a little while. The idea of fluffy dogs and cats seemed soothing, and that's just what she needed right now.

The shelter wasn't far from Joss' house, so she decided to walk after checking the weather app on her phone. It called for rain, but it was a slim chance, so she figured she'd carry her umbrella and hope for the best. She walked slowly, enjoying the neighborhood that she'd lived in for the last seven years. It was easy to let her mind begin to worry about what was going to happen with her living situation. She loved the area, and her neighbors, and wasn't sure that she wanted to leave at all. Joss made a promise to herself to work out some numbers to see if there was any possible way for her to purchase the home from Brandon herself. As she tried calculating the details in her mind, Joss stopped walking. The shelter was up one more street, but Natasha's house was to the left. She didn't want to be weird or morbid, but she wanted to see the house. Making the turn, she walked down High Street, pausing in front of Natasha's home.

The crime scene tape was down, and the house looked silent. The lawn was a bit overgrown, and there were items placed near the mailbox and on the porch. Things like stuffed animals, candles, signs, and cards were laid everywhere. Joss couldn't help but remember the night of the catering event. Andy had told Crystal that he was there for a memorial for a coworker. Joss realized the irony of it all, seeing everything set-up to memorialize Natasha. She knelt, looking at the things that were laid behind the mailbox, thinking that she should have sent some flowers or something. Soon, if not already, Andy would be back at the house. She wasn't sure if he'd be living there or not, but someone would have to go through everything of Natasha's.

Life had been so crazy for Joss lately, but nothing compared to losing someone you loved. She felt for Andy, and Judy, and Natasha's grandfather. She made a mental note to talk to Jack as soon as she could, thanking him for coming to her. Without that bit of information, who knows what would have happened to Andy.

Apparently, Joss had spent more time at Natasha's than she planned, either that or the weatherman was wrong, because the rain was already starting. Suddenly, in the midst of a downpour, and an umbrella that refused to open, Joss dashed under the carport on the side driveway. She needed shelter and would try to stay there until the rain passed, or she could get her umbrella to function properly. Messing with the button that made the umbrella pop up, Joss squeezed it too hard, and a piece of the plastic broke, flying across the ground. She took a few steps, trying to retrieve it when she saw something that made her shudder.

A bicycle with a piece of red linen in the chain. Red linen that matched the diner's table runners. Joss got closer, bending down to look at the bike, being cautious as not to touch anything, when she heard someone let out a laugh. Maniacal as it was, Joss turned. She was face to face with Marni, Judy and Natasha's assistant.

"What are you doing here?" Marni asked.

"I could ask you the same thing," Joss challenged. "Have you seen this bike? It has something on it, and I'm worried it has something to do with Natasha's murder. Do you know who it belongs to?"

"You just don't give up, do you? I suppose it's a good quality to have. Maybe not in this situation." Marni snickered.

"I want to make sure nothing was missed. What if..."

"You think I haven't been keeping an eye on you all this time? I tried planting the seed. Tried telling you that Judy and Natasha were fighting, but it didn't stick. No. You had to traipse around looking for more clues. I thought for sure you'd blame the wife, because well, who wouldn't in this situation? Then, when I told Gloria that I thought it was Andy, she went off all crazy, and I thought that would stop you. But here you are. Still not giving up." Marni stepped closer, wet hair in her face and make-up streaking down her cheeks.

"What are you talking about? I'm not here looking for clues. I was walking by and decided to stop to look at everything that people put here for Natasha," Joss asked, backing up. "What are you doing here, Marni?"

"Picking up my bike," she replied, an evil look coming over her face.

"Your bike?" Joss asked, heart pounding. "Are you saying what I think you're saying?"

The rain was beginning to slow and Joss wasn't sure

if she should run or try to protect herself in case Marni was planning something.

"Don't be dumb. Of course I am. I hated Natasha. She didn't want Judy to hire me. She wouldn't let me make any jewelry unless she designed it and approved the pieces after the fact, and even if she deemed them worthy, I still wasn't allowed to sell them under her name. She was using company money for private things, and she walked all over Judy. It wasn't fair, and Judy was nothing but kind to me from the beginning. Natasha had it coming. If I didn't kill her, someone else would have." Marni raced toward Joss; hand raised.

"Joss! Duck!" Dina screamed.

Joss acted fast and did what she was told, watching Marni get hit and fall to the ground in pain. She took her phone, calling the emergency number she knew all too well.

CHAPTER EIGHTEEN

"Dina, come in," Joss said, gesturing to her living room.

"Thanks. I wasn't sure you'd let me." Dina stepped passed Joss.

"Are you kidding? Who would have thought that one of those crazy things you wear on your feet would have saved my life?" Joss chuckled. "You're always welcome here."

"It's not nice to tease people, ya know," Dina said, smiling. "I'm glad you're okay."

"Me, too. How did you know I'd be there?" Joss asked. "Please tell me you weren't following me again. I mean, I'm happy you were there and all, but watching people is kinda creepy."

"I wasn't. I was driving to your house and took a wrong turn because the rain was so bad. I didn't even know you were there at first. It wasn't until I pulled over to wait out the storm when I saw you. When the rain started to slow down, I got out to talk to you, and when I saw that woman charge at you, I knew I had to do something."

"You really saved me," Joss said gratefully.

"Right place, right time, is all." Dina shrugged.

"Wait a minute. Why were you going to my house? You haven't spoken to me in over a week."

"I was feeling guilty. You have to leave your house, the woman you did a catering job for was killed, and to think, had I not been acting like a five-year-old, it would have been my catering job. I just felt bad I guess, and I wanted to apologize to you for acting that way."

Joss put her arm around Dina. "That's kind of you. I appreciate the apology and you saving me from Marni. It was a crazy day for sure. I can't believe she was the one that killed Natasha."

"Did you ever hear anything more about it?" Dina asked.

Joss nodded. "The night of the event, after everyone left, Andy went back to talk to Natasha but saw Judy's car there and didn't want to talk with her there. It turned out that Judy was there but not consoling Natasha like I originally thought. She left the house after I did to pick up Marni who was upset after not being invited to the event. She'd had a few too many drinks to console herself, and needed a ride home. After Judy got her, she had to stop back by Natasha's because she forgot her purse and didn't want to be driving without her license. Marni was still with her, and she claimed she had to use the restroom. She went into the house, unbeknownst to Natasha, telling Judy she locked the door behind her. I guess she never really locked it and ended up coming back later that night to kill her."

"Wow," Dina said, shaking her head in disbelief. "She admitted all of that?"

"I guess she lost control and couldn't hold it all in any longer. I'm just surprised she wasn't a little more careful. When I saw her bike with a piece of the table runner on it, I couldn't believe she didn't notice it, or if she did, why she'd leave it there like a souvenir or something."

"What a crazy thing. I'm sorry it all happened to you."

"Thanks," Joss said, smiling.

"That's what friends are for," Dina said.

"Are we friends again?" Joss asked.

"I saved your life, Joss. You owe me." Dina grinned.

"You owe me a shift at work, then. Remember the day you walked out? You're lucky you weren't fired."

"I know. I know. I was wrong; you don't have to rub it in," Dina said, sticking out her tongue. "So, what are you doing for the rest of the day? Want to do something?"

"I'm supposed to hang out with Ryan, but..."

"Okay. Cool. I get it. You should definitely see him. We can make plans for some other time," Dina said quickly.

"Actually, I have an idea. Ryan and I are thinking of going to check out the new theme park that opened a couple of hours away. How about you come with us?" Joss asked.

"And be the third wheel? I don't think that sounds like a very good idea." Dina frowned.

"What about if Richie comes too?"

"What?!" Dina shouted. "Why would you even suggest that?"

"Oh, come on. You know you like him," Joss said.

"I mean, maybe a little. But there is no way he feels the same. We are two totally different people."

"That's what makes the world go round, Dina. We all like different things, and have different beliefs and that's okay. You'll never know unless you try. I asked Ryan out, remember? If I can do it, so can you."

"I don't know," Dina said, sounding unsure.

"You got this. I'm not worried at all. I'm almost positive he'll say yes."

"Really?" Dina asked, perking up.

"How about you call him and find out? I'll call Ryan and let him know and we can go on a double date. It'll be fun!"

"Thanks, Joss," Dina said.

"Anything for a friend," Joss replied, giving Dina the biggest smile she could.

Life was back to normal for Joss, and it felt good. She couldn't wait to see Ryan, and get back to work now that Dina was speaking to her again. The next time someone said she had to do a catering job by herself, though, she was definitely going to decline.

————

The next morning, Joss stepped into the diner, rubbing her tired eyes. She'd stayed up late watching movies with Ryan and it was one of the best, and most relaxing nights she'd had in a long time, so it had been more than worth it. She went straight to the coffee pot, and poured herself a cup. Walking into the kitchen, Joss removed the special coffee creamer that she stored at the diner from the fridge, and laughed out loud. On the bottle was a bright pink sticky note, no doubt from Dina.

Richie said YES!

ALSO BY GRETCHEN ALLEN

Sundae Afternoon Series

Book 1: Triple Dipped Murder

Book 2: Melt Down Murder

Book 3: A Twist of Murder

Book 4: Caked in Murder

Book 5: Shivers of Murder

Book 6: A Flurry of Murder

Book 7: Two Scoops of Murder

The Day and Night Diner

Book 1: Pancakes and Pleas

The Cozy Tales of a Professional Mermaid

Book 1: Criminals and Coral

Holly and Evergreen

Book 1: The Final Sleigh

AUTHOR'S NOTE

I'd love to hear your thoughts on my books, the storylines, and anything else that you'd like to comment on—reader feedback is very important to me. My contact information, along with some other helpful links, is listed on the next page. If you'd like to be on my list of "folks to contact" with updates, release and sales notifications, etc.... just shoot me an email and let me know. Thanks for reading!

Also...

... if you're looking for more great reads, I am proud to announce that Summer Prescott Books publishes several popular series by Cozy authors Summer Prescott and Patti Benning, as well as Allyssa Mirry, Blair Merrin, Susie Gayle and more!

CONTACT SUMMER PRESCOTT BOOKS PUBLISHING

Follow Gretchen on Facebook!

Twitter: @summerprescottı

Blog and Book Catalog: http://summerprescottbooks.com

Email: summer.prescott.cozies@gmail.com

And...look up The Summer Prescott Fan Page and Summer Prescott Publishing Page on Facebook – let's be friends!

To download a free book, and sign up for our fun and exciting newsletter, which will give you opportunities to win prizes and swag, enter contests, and be the first to know about New Releases, click here: http://summerprescottbooks.com

Made in the USA
Monee, IL
05 January 2025